The Very Best Christmas Present

By Jim Razzi

Illustrated by Henry Fernandes

To my daughter Jennifer—J.R.

A Golden Book • New York

Western Publishing Company, Inc., Racine, Wisconsin 53404

One snowy morning, a few weeks before Christmas, Mr. Floogle's doorbell rang. It was the mail carrier. He had a big orange cat in his arms.

"Is this your cat?" asked the mail carrier. "I found it in your mailbox."

"No," said Mr. Floogle, "I live alone. And, furthermore, I don't like cats."

"Meow," said the cat, looking cold and sad.

"I can't keep it," said the mail carrier.

"Oh, bother," said Mr. Floogle. Then he looked at the cat.

"Meow," said the cat, looking back with big yellow eyes.

"Well, I guess I can keep it for today," said Mr. Floogle, "but tomorrow it must go."

Mr. Floogle took the cat in and gave it a saucer of milk. Then he went about his chores.

"Meow," said the cat as Mr. Floogle washed the dishes.

"It's no use trying to talk to me," said Mr. Floogle. "I don't like cats."

So the cat kept quiet and just watched.

Mr. Floogle whistled while he washed the dishes.

"That's funny," he said to himself, "I haven't whistled in years!"

The day passed, and it was time to go to bed. The cat curled up beside Mr. Floogle and said, "Meow."

"It's no use trying to talk to me," said Mr. Floogle. "I don't like cats."

So the cat just lay there, purring gently.

The purring put Mr. Floogle to sleep as soon as he closed his eyes.

The next morning Mr. Floogle took the cat out in his car and drove to a dairy farm nearby.

"This is where I will leave you. You'll like it here," Mr. Floogle said.

"I just don't like cats," Mr. Floogle said to himself as he drove away.

Mr. Floogle went to bed that night and said, "That's that!" But the next morning, very early, the doorbell rang.

It was the dairy farmer. He had a big orange cat in his arms.

"Is this your cat?" asked the dairy farmer. "I found it in one of my empty milk cans."

"No," said Mr. Floogle, who was surprised to see the cat again. "I don't like cats."

"Meow," said the cat, looking hopeful.

"I can't keep it," said the dairy farmer.

"Oh, bother," said Mr. Floogle.

Then he looked at the cat. The cat looked back and purred.

"Well, I suppose I can keep it for today," said Mr. Floogle with a sigh, "but tomorrow it must go."

Mr. Floogle took the cat in and gave it a scrambled egg for breakfast. Then he went to sit in his chair.

"Meow," said the cat as it played with Mr. Floogle's robe.

"It's no use trying to play with me," said Mr. Floogle. "I don't like cats."

So the cat just played with a piece of paper as Mr. Floogle watched.

"Silly cat," he said to himself.

The next day Mr. Floogle took the cat out in the car again. "I will take you far away this time so that you won't come back," he said.

Mr. Floogle drove and drove until he came to a flying school. There were several other cats around. "You'll have plenty of company here," said Mr. Floogle.

"Meow," said the cat.

"No, you can't stay with me," answered Mr. Floogle. "I told you, I don't like cats."

Mr. Floogle left the cat at the flying school and drove home again. "That's that!" he said.

The next morning, while Mr. Floogle was working on his house, someone jumped right onto his roof! It was a sky diver. She had a big orange cat in her arms.

"Is this your cat?" asked the sky diver. "It jumped right out of the plane with me as we flew over your house."

"No," said Mr. Floogle, rolling his eyes. "It's not my cat, it never was my cat, and I don't want it to be my cat!"

"Well, I can't keep it," said the sky diver. "And, anyway, it seems to like you."

"Meow," said the cat, looking at Mr. Floogle lovingly.

"Oh, bother," Mr. Floogle said with a sigh.

"Well, I guess I'll have to keep you for today," he said, "but tomorrow you must go for good!" Mr. Floogle went back to his work.

"Meow," said the cat as it lay in the sun.

"Oh, really?" said Mr. Floogle. "Well, I didn't miss you."

"Meow," said the cat softly.

"Stuff and nonsense," said Mr. Floogle.

The next morning Mr. Floogle looked at the cat and said, "I really must get rid of you today. You know I don't like cats."

He thought and thought about what to do. All of a sudden Mr. Floogle had the best idea of all!

"Since you were found in my mailbox," he said, "I will let the post office take care of it!"

That very same day Mr. Floogle took the cat to the post office.

"I want to mail this cat somewhere far, far away," he said to the postal clerk.

"How about the North Pole?" said the postal clerk. "That's far, far away, and we have a nice warm post office there."

Mr. Floogle looked down at the cat. The cat reached up and licked his face.

"Stuff and nonsense," said Mr. Floogle as he wiped off the kiss.

Then, without knowing why, he suddenly asked, "Will they take good care of it at the North Pole Post Office?"

"Of course," answered the postal clerk, looking offended. "We always take good care of the mail—especially at Christmastime!"

And, without another word, he took the cat into the package room.

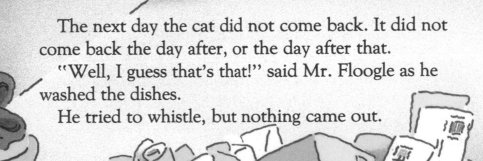

The next day the cat did not come back. It did not come back the day after, or the day after that.

"Well, I guess that's that!" said Mr. Floogle as he washed the dishes.

He tried to whistle, but nothing came out.

More days passed, and still the cat did not come back.

"Well," said Mr. Floogle, a little quietly, "I guess that's that."

He climbed into bed, but for some reason he couldn't fall asleep.

"Stuff and nonsense," he murmured. "I'm just not tired."

Now, it just so happened that the next day was Christmas Eve. Mr. Floogle watched from his window as people hurried to and fro, their arms filled with presents.

"Stuff and nonsense," he sniffed. Mr. Floogle didn't have any friends, so he never expected any presents for Christmas.

Just then, for no good reason, he thought of the cat. "I wonder what that silly cat is doing now," he mused as he sat in his chair. "It's a good thing I don't like cats," he said to himself, "or I might miss it."

Just before midnight Mr. Floogle went to bed. But when he got under the covers, he tossed and turned and couldn't get to sleep.

When he finally did go to sleep, he started to dream. He dreamed that he was doing his chores and the cat was watching him. He dreamed that he was sitting in his chair and the cat was playing with his robe. He dreamed that he was in bed and the cat was purring beside him. He smiled to himself and reached over to pet it...

Then he woke up and remembered that the cat was gone. All of a sudden he felt very sad and lonely.

"Stuff and nonsense," he whispered as he laid his head upon his pillow. "I don't even like cats."

Just then someone rang his doorbell. He ran down to answer it.

It was Santa Claus!

He had a big orange cat in his arms.

"Is this your cat?" asked Santa. "I found it hiding in my sled at the North Pole."

Mr. Floogle had been so used to saying no that he almost said it again.

But suddenly he cried, "Yes—yes! It is my cat!"

"Meow," said the cat.

"I'm glad you're back, too," said Mr. Floogle, stroking the cat's soft fur.

Then Mr. Floogle turned to Santa.

"But how did you know it was my cat?" he asked.

Instead of answering, Santa just gave Mr. Floogle a wink and a nod and hopped into his sled.

Mr. Floogle waved good-bye as Santa's sled disappeared over the treetops.

"Meow," said the cat.

"I missed you, too," said Mr. Floogle.

"Meow," said the cat.

"Merry Christmas to you, too," answered Mr. Floogle as he gave his cat a big hug. "You're the best Christmas present I could ever want."